SMITTY HITS THE BOOKS
^Play

WADE SMITH & JAYME LAMM
illustrations by JAMES LITTLE

bright sky press
HOUSTON, TEXAS

DEDICATION
To my wife Rita, and my girls Arissa, Aaliyah & Arielle.
Hope you are proud of Daddy...It's all for you.

And to every child that reads this story, dream big, set goals,
believe in yourself, do your best and DON'T FORGET YOUR HOMEWORK!

ACKNOWLEDGMENTS
Special thanks to Mama & Pop. You laid the foundation
and gave me guidance throughout my life.
Love you always.

To Lake Highlands, Texas...Forever in debt to the community that I love.

To Jayme & James, we did it! This wouldn't be possible without your
vision, talent and hard work. Salute!

To Gabrielle, your input, insight and perspective was invaluable
throughout this process. Thank you.

To Annie Mae, I miss you, our talks and your laugh. Even though you are gone,
thank you for reminding me each and every day that God is Love.

bright sky press
HOUSTON, TEXAS

2365 Rice Blvd., Suite 202
Houston, Texas 77005

ISBN: 978-1-942945-33-8

10   9   8   7   6   5   4   3   2

Library of Congress Cataloging-in-Publication Data on file with publisher.

Editorial Direction: Lucy Herring Chambers
Managing Editor: Lauren Gow
Designer: Marla Y. Garcia

Production Date: March 2016
Batch Number: 55692-0
Plant Location: Printed by We SP Corp., Seoul, Korea

Since he was very little, Smitty dreamed of playing football. He watched the older kids in the neighborhood passing and catching, and he knew he wanted to play just like those guys—maybe even better!

He longed to play for the Pop Warner Wildcats. During school he doodled their logo and drew his favorite players. He imagined their touchdown celebrations—he had practiced his own for years!

One year for Christmas, his mom gave him a Lake Highlands High School Wildcat varsity football jersey. It was Smitty's first jersey, and it made him feel like a real football player!

He wore it everywhere—to school, to church...

... and even to Penny Whistle Park. He wore it until it didn't fit anymore.

Smitty knew he belonged on the football field. But his mom wouldn't let him play. She thought it was a dangerous sport, meant for bigger boys. Smitty was tall but very skinny, and his mom thought he might get hurt.

When the week of tryouts came, Smitty had to convince his mom to let him play.

He promised her that he'd be very safe. He'd wear all the protective gear and do everything his coaches told him to. He begged and pleaded, and finally his mom agreed. Smitty was finally ready to live his dream!

It was finally happening! After school a few days later, Smitty put on his cleats and pads, his practice jersey and his helmet and headed out to the field. He loved playing with the kids in his neighborhood, but this was real football. Smitty wanted to make his mom proud.

It didn't take long. Smitty was a natural. He wasn't as big and strong as some of the other kids, but he was super fast. No one on the other teams could keep up with him. And, he was tall—he could leap over everyone on the defense and catch the ball! He scored a touchdown at almost every practice.

Like many kids, Smitty thought about football so much that he ignored his schoolwork. Each night his teacher, Ms. Hart, would assign math problems, spelling words and reading assignments, but all he could think about was what a great player he would be one day. He just stopped doing his homework.

When Ms. Hart called on him, he became the class clown. He told her that the dog ate his homework. Everyone around him would laugh.

Smitty didn't even have a dog!

His mom always told him how important school was. But she worked long hours to be the best mom she could be, and she didn't know that Smitty was out playing football every afternoon instead of doing his work. But one person knew, and she didn't think it was funny.

Ms. Hart never laughed when Smitty made jokes about his homework. She was always very patient with her students, no matter how much they acted up in class. Smitty loved his mom so much, and at school he looked up to Ms. Hart almost like she was another parent. He wanted to please them, but football was so exciting!

Now, football was all Smitty could think about. He daydreamed about football even more than he did before. It got so bad that Ms. Hart had to call his mom.

Smitty was in for a big surprise...

The Wednesday before his next big game, Smitty's mom looked very serious when she sat at the dinner table.

"Ms. Hart says you've missed three homework assignments in a row and your grades are going down!" she scolded. "Until you start studying again and show me that you deserve to play football, you're not allowed to play."

Smitty begged for another chance, but his mom meant business.

Smitty could barely sleep that night. Football was his life, and now his mom wouldn't let him play!

The next day at school was long and terrible. When the final bell rang, all his buddies went to the field. Smitty had to stay in study hall.

"It isn't fair!" he thought. "I should be outside playing football too!"

For a few days Smitty sulked. Then something clicked in his mind. It felt great to make his coaches and teammates proud, but if it took up all his school time, he was disappointing his mom and Ms. Hart. The other kids on his team turned in their homework. If they found time to do it all, then so could Smitty!

That very second Smitty knew that if he wanted to keep playing football, school had to come first.

He started working as hard at school as he did at football. It took focus and determination—plus tons of extra reading—but Smitty got his grades up. He missed six practices and two whole games!

During that time Ms. Hart and Smitty's mom had regular phone calls about his progress. Even the principal checked in on him.

After the math test, Ms. Hart called Smitty's mother. "I'm really proud of him," Ms. Hart said. "He got the highest score in the class on the test."

"I think he finally realizes how important schoolwork is," his mother said, "especially if he wants to become a great football player one day."

That very second Smitty's mom and Ms. Hart agreed he had worked so hard that it was time to let him play football again—as long as he promised to keep up with his schoolwork and pay attention during class!

When his mother told him the good news, you could see the twinkle in Smitty's eyes from a mile away—even through his glasses! His hard work had paid off!

During those weeks in study hall, Smitty had missed out on what was happening on the field. A lot had changed. He hadn't heard the new plays, and the team had gotten a new quarterback. Smitty had been a star, but now he had to sit on the sidelines and patiently wait to get in the game.

He decided to work even harder to show his coach, Ms. Hart and especially his mom he could do it all. It wasn't easy, but Smitty's mom had always taught him he could do anything he set his mind to doing.

Smitty was focused and determined. It wasn't long before he was back on the field scoring touchdowns. But now, he was also making A's and B's on his schoolwork. He was doing all his regular homework and every extra credit assignment Ms. Hart gave the class. She noticed a big change in Smitty's attitude, and she liked it.

Soon, Smitty had a new routine that made time for studying and practicing. Thanks to his mom and Ms. Hart, he had learned a very valuable lesson—

NO HOMEWORK = NO FOOTBALL!

And Smitty never wanted to have to live without playing football again!

THE WADE SMITH FOUNDATION

Founded in 2012 by twelve-year NFL veteran, Houston Texans Pro Bowl player and Dallas-native Wade Smith. The Wade Smith Foundation (WSF) provides support for youth and community programs in childhood literacy and education, an annual scholarship program and both memorable experiences and opportunities to cultivate and encourage the dreams and goals of deserving children and families.

The foundation's Reading with the Pros literacy program (RWTP) features in-person celebrity book readings and classroom visits. To date, more than sixty current and former NFL players and college athletes have joined Wade at more than twenty RWTP reading events at public libraries and elementary schools throughout Houston and Dallas, Texas. Reading with the Pros has shared the importance of reading and education with over 22,000 elementary-age students and public library visitors.

When asked about the children he hopes RWTP will impact, Wade says, "Whether it comes easy for them, or they need help from a parent, friend, tutor or teacher, *everyone* has the ability to become better readers and find topics in books that are fun and interesting to them."

Since its inception in 2012, The Wade Smith Foundation has provided over $80,000 in scholarships. The WSF Scholarship program "Smitty's Scholars" awards a minimum of $20,000 annually to outgoing high school seniors in Dallas and Houston, Texas. These scholarships are merit-based awards that focus on the recipients' academic performance with a strong emphasis on community involvement.

To learn more about all the ways The Wade Smith Foundation is working to help improve children's lives through literacy or to make a charitable donation, please visit *www.WadeSmithFoundation.org.*